Pete the Cat

Rocking in My
School Shoes

B 2024

3

For Dr Stephen Litwin, my father,
who told me my first stories
— E.L.

To Kim, the girl who told me she wanted to live in a small
cabin and make things out of clay
— J.D.

First published in hardback by HarperCollins Publishers, USA, in 2011
First published in paperback in Great Britain by HarperCollins Children's Books in 2015

1 3 5 7 9 10 8 6 4 2

ISBN: 978-0-00-755365-5

HarperCollins Children's Books is a division of HarperCollins Publishers Ltd.
Visit our website at www.harpercollins.co.uk
Printed and bound in China

Pete the Cat
Rocking in My School Shoes

Story by
Eric Litwin

Art by
James Dean
(creator of Pete the Cat)

HarperCollins *Children's Books*

Here comes Pete
strolling down the street,
rocking red shoes
on his four furry feet.

Pete is going to school,
and he sings this song:

PETE'S
LUNCH

"I'm rocking in my **school** shoes,

I'm rocking in my **school** shoes,

I'm rocking in my **school** shoes."

Pete is sitting at his desk when his teacher says, "Come on, Pete, down that hall to a room with books on every wall."

Pete has never been to the library before!

Does Pete worry?
Goodness, no!

He finds his favourite book
and sings his song:

"I'm reading in my **school** shoes,

I'm reading in my **school** shoes,

I'm reading in my **school** shoes."

Check out Pete.
He's ready to eat
in a big, noisy room
with tables and seats.

Where is Pete?

The lunchroom!

It can be loud and busy in the lunchroom.

Does Pete worry?
Goodness, no!

He sits down with his friends
and sings his song:

"I'm eating in my **school** shoes,

I'm eating in my **school** shoes,

I'm eating in my **school** shoes."

Pete and his friends
        are playing outside
            on a green, grassy field
                with swings and tall slides.

Where is Pete?

The playground!

Kids are running in every direction!

Does Pete worry?

Goodness, no!

He slides, and swings, and sings his song:

"I'm playing in my **school** shoes,

I'm playing in my **school** shoes,

I'm playing in my **school** shoes."

All day long Pete sings his song.

"I'm singing in my **school** shoes,

I'm painting in my **school** shoes,

I'm adding in my **school** shoes,

I'm writing in my **school** shoes."

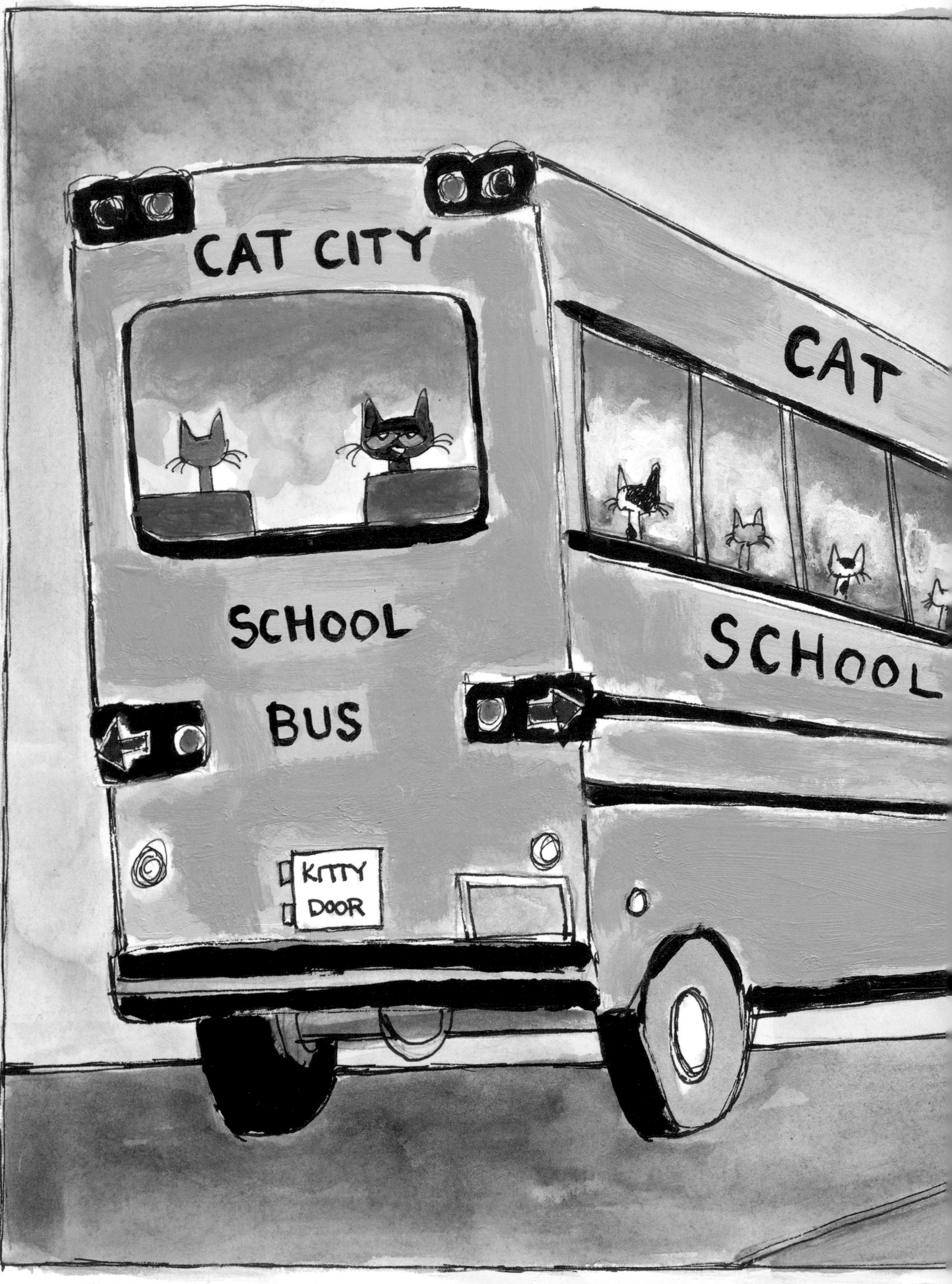
CAT CITY
SCHOOL
BUS
KITTY
DOOR
CAT
SCHOOL

When school is done, Pete rides the bus home.

"I was rocking in my **school** shoes,

I was rocking in my **school** shoes,

I was rocking in my **school** shoes.

And I will do it
again tomorrow!

Because it's all good."

Don't be sad! There's more Pete the Cat to read!

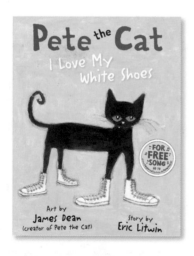

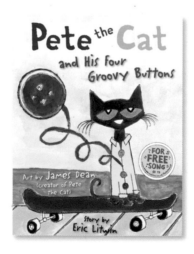

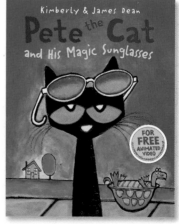